Each Puffin Easy-to-Read book has a color-coded reading level to make book selection easy for parents and children. Because all children are unique in their reading development, Puffin's three levels make it easy for teachers and parents to find the right book to suit each individual child's reading readiness.

Level 1:   Short, simple sentences full of word repetition—plus clear visual clues to help children take the first important steps toward reading.

Level 2:   More words and longer sentences for children just beginning to read on their own.

Level 3:   Lively, fast-paced text—perfect for children who are reading on their own.

"Readers aren't born, they're made.
Desire is planted—planted by
parents who work at it."

—Jim Trelease, author of
The Read-Aloud Handbook

For Jason and Lucy
S.T.

PUFFIN BOOKS
Published by the Penguin Group
Penguin Books USA Inc., 375 Hudson Street, New York, New York 10014, U.S.A.
Penguin Books Ltd, 27 Wrights Lane, London W8 5TZ, England
Penguin Books Australia Ltd, Ringwood, Victoria, Australia
Penguin Books Canada Ltd, 10 Alcorn Avenue, Toronto, Ontario, Canada M4V 3B2
Penguin Books (N.Z.) Ltd, 182–190 Wairau Road, Auckland 10, New Zealand

Penguin Books Ltd, Registered Offices: Harmondsworth, Middlesex, England

First published in the United States of America by Viking Penguin Inc., 1987
Simultaneously published in Puffin Books
Published in a Puffin Easy-to-Read edition, 1993

5 7 9 10 8 6

LIBRARY OF CONGRESS CATALOGING-IN-PUBLICATION DATA

Ziefert, Harriet.
Jason's bus ride / Harriet Ziefert;
pictures by Simms Taback.   p.   cm. — (Puffin easy-to-read)
"Reading level 1.6" — T.p. verso.
"First published in the United States of America
by Viking Penguin Inc., 1987" — T.p. verso.
Summary: Jason becomes a hero when he takes a bus ride.
ISBN 0-14-036536-2
[1. Buses—Fiction.]
I. Taback, Simms, ill. II. Title III. Series.
[PZ7.Z487Jas   1993]
[E]—dc20   93-2723   CIP   AC

Puffin® and Easy-to-Read® are registered trademarks of Penguin Books USA Inc.
Printed in the United States of America

Reading Level 1.6

Jason's Bus Ride

Harriet Ziefert
Illustrated by Simms Taback

PUFFIN BOOKS

Jason got on the bus.

He paid the bus driver.

Then he found a good seat.

Jason looked around.

There were all kinds
of people on the bus.

There were all kinds
of people outside.

Jason saw cars and trucks
and bikes and motorcycles.

All of a sudden
the bus stopped.

"Why did we stop?"
Jason asked.

A man said, "The bus stopped
because of a dog. The dog
is in front of the bus."

The dog would not move.
He would not get out
of the way.

The bus driver
beeped his horn.

But the dog would not
get out of the way!

A lady shouted,
"Shoo! Shoo!"

But the dog would not
get out of the way!

A policeman blew his whistle.

But the dog would not get out of the way!

A man and a lady
pulled the dog.

But the dog would not
get out of the way!

A lady with a crying baby
walked up to the dog.

The lady said, "Move away!
My baby wants to go home."

But the dog would not
get out of the way!

Everyone watched.
Everyone waited.

Jason patted the dog.
Good dog! Good dog!

The dog smiled.

Then he walked away.

Jason got back on the bus.

Everyone clapped.

Hooray! Hooray!
They all drove away!